HELLO, HEDGEHOG!™

Do You Like My Bike?

Norm Feuti

ACORN™
SCHOLASTIC INC.

For Mom —NF

Library of Congress Cataloging-in-Publication Data

Names: Feuti, Norman, author.
Title: Do you like my bike? / by Norm Feuti.
Description: First edition. | New York, NY : Scholastic Inc., [2019] |
Series: Hello, Hedgehog! ; 1 | Summary: Hedgehog goes riding on his new
bike, with his best friend Harry.
Identifiers: LCCN 2018035379| ISBN 9781338281385 (pbk. : alk. paper) | ISBN
9781338281392 (hardcover : alk. paper)
Subjects: LCSH: Bicycles—Juvenile fiction. | Cycling—Juvenile fiction. |
Best friends—Juvenile fiction. | Friendship—Juvenile fiction. | CYAC:
Bicycles and bicycling—Fiction. | Best friends—Fiction. |
Friendship—Fiction. | Hedgehogs—Fiction.
Classification: LCC PZ7.1.F52 Do 2019 | DDC [E]—dc23
LC record available at https://lccn.loc.gov/ 2018035379

10 9 8 7 6 5 4 3 2 1   19 20 21 22 23
Printed in China   62
First edition, May 2019
Edited by Katie Carella
Book design by Maria Mercado

Lost Helmet

I have a new bike!
I cannot wait to ride it!

8

13

14

20

22

Ring!
Ring!
Ring!
Ring!
Ring!
Ring!
Ring!

H'HOG

37

39

40

41

43

About the Author

Norm Feuti lives in Massachusetts with his family, a dog, two cats, and a guinea pig. He is the creator of the newspaper comic strips **Retail** and **Gil**. He is also the author and illustrator of the graphic novel **The King of Kazoo**. **Hello, Hedgehog!** is Norm's first early reader series.

YOU CAN DRAW HEDGEHOG!

1. Draw a jelly bean shape.

2. Draw the nose and eyes.

3. Add ears and lots of quills!

4. Draw little arms and hands. Add legs and feet, too!

5. Put black spots on the ends of the quills. Finish the face.

6. Color in your drawing!

WHAT'S YOUR STORY?

Hedgehog goes bike riding with Harry.
Imagine Hedgehog asks **you** to go bike riding.
What would your bike look like?
Where would you and Hedgehog go?
Write and draw your story!